I0744973

ISBN : 978-1-911424-82-6
SKU/ID: 9781911424826

A catalogue record for this book is available from the British Library.

English translation: Francesca Raffaelli
Text revision: Monica Turoni
Editor: Monica Turoni
Cover and Book design: Wolf Graham

Publishing Company:
Black Wolf Edition & Publishing Ltd.
Scotland
www.blackwolfedition.com

VITTORIO GRAZIOSI

BLOOD OF SCARLET ROSE

(The Diary)

July-August 2005

(7th July, 2005)

My hands were dipped in lather that felt like creamy clouds. It was an ordinary day, I was such in a good mood that everything seemed even better. Finally, some good news.

"Pa, I will come back home tonight. Will you prepare some tortellini with cream and olive ascolane?" Here is the first morning of this story or the last of my life. Memories and reality are confused like some disinfectant with blood on a wound. I believe I replied laughing, "I certainly will, your Majesty. I will lay the table for the best banquet of the year to welcome your return."

I was monkeying about with a cue, but I meant it completely. He was my life. He grew up in my arms...

I bite my lips in anger. He grew up in a blink. I remember he was a rosy and chubby baby, perfumed like powder-puff.

Now, he is a palm taller than me; fair and soft hairs on his chin keep myself from smothering him with kisses.

I am trying to recall all the steps of his growth and yet how he became a man in an instant remains a magnificent mystery. Thus, I found myself from baby food to take care of a man. Always with the same love I had the first time, when his mother put him in my arms. His mother, indeed! We haven't seen her so often since then. She thought she was not suitable to be a mother. She used to say she wanted to "live a life in each continent".

However, this is a different story.

Time has gone, when I recall that cursed day I can feel the intense stroke on my chest, right on my heart. I felt my ribs shacking. I don't remember any other sign. Maybe this is how a premonition works.

That morning I had the radio on a modern music channel. I couldn't sing the melody but it was captivating, I was tuning up some invented words. I was washing the dishes and singing. I was singing to conceal my mental activity. I usually do that when my son is away. Anxiety is a cold snake that runs on your back, somehow I had to tame it. The music suddenly stops and I already know I will receive a deadly blow. I can feel my organs shattering. I feel sick.

"Breaking news... Breaking news... A new terrorist attack!!! The heart of London was attacked. Three bombs hit public transportation and exploded in rapid progression. We will provide more detailed news shortly."

My God! My beloved son! God, let me die now!!! Drown my memory in the sea. Let the mud of my fear choke me. I cling on to the edge of the sink not to fall.

I don't know why I don't call him.

I call the school office. Then the Farnesina but the line is busy; finally, they pick it up. They know nothing. They will call me back. Then, I turn off everything. Radio, TV, lights and I am waiting in a corner next to the telephone. I wait in the semi-darkness despite it is morning, despite the sunlight.

I am afraid of the world's indifference to this lucid insanity.

I am even scared of the shadows that move in this

room, allowing time to pass while waiting for the telephone to ring.

I am worried my heart will survive to bad news. It is almost evening but the telephone has not rung yet...

No more shadows are around, a sunset dust covers everything and all seems unreal.

The clock ticking brings me back to reality. I can't bear this any longer. I want some news! I start screaming.

The doorbell, covered by my screams, rings. He has to insist, I finally hear it. I drag myself to the door.

A lieutenant of the Carabinieri stands in front of me, he greets me and asks to talk to Paolo's father. I would never get into that conversation... I hesitate. I wished I could cheat destiny.

"It's me..."

"Unfortunately your son did not survive. He is one of the victims caused by the first bomb in London's underground. I am very sorry."

I knew it, damn it! I knew it; I was not able to die with him. I do not fall on the ground as I wished.

"His body will be brought back to Italy the day after tomorrow by noon. If you want, we can take you to Rome to receive your son's remains."

Bombe nel metrò e sull'autobus
Mattinata di terrore nei sotterranei: decine di morti
La sequenza delle esplosioni
UNDERGROUND
Al Qaida rivendica l'attentato
Tra le centinaia di feriti anche due italiani

(9th July, 2005)

The following two days pass in clear insanity. I prepare some tortellini with cream sauce and olive ascolane as he had asked me. I set the table and let them cool down there, in silence. Then I throw everything away. I don't turn on TV or listen to radio. I don't even answer the telephone that keeps on ringing all day long. I don't care to known who could be. My son is dead!

I am at the airport's morgue. He is in front of me. I am calmer now. No, it is not true! I stare at his mouth. I imagine words behind his shut lips. I touch his cold hand and I close my eyes. But the miracle of finding myself in his place will not happen. I lost a son and my son lost me. I have lived with his heartbeats and died with his last one. The end. Unfortunately, it won't be like this. I feel the hands "of the people of men", a different race, touching my shoulders as they want to comfort me. A magic caress to save me from the whirlpool. Damn you all! Leave me alone, I want to go down to the Scheol. I want my son anywhere that damned bomb took him. I am holding my breath... I resist...resist...resist...then I bite my lips until they bleed. I feel dizzy and a breath of air ends my endurance. I want my affliction. I am pain stricken, such a painful misery that my bones hurt. I am so insane that I feel serene knowing that a tombstone is now protecting him.

Small sunbeams tinkle on the golden initials of his name and I touch them lightly to feel the warm spirit of God. His touch is in the morning wind.

How can I live now that I am dead too? I hear

some of his friends talking but I don't let them come in. I look indecent and unpresentable. A deep sorrow is always discomposed. Dead sorrow stinks, it's disgusting! I am waiting in darkness and silence. Soon or later, my heart has to understand it has gone over its last heartbeat.

(20th August, 2005)

I have already lived thousand years of deep sighs, I have shed tears and I have cried again. Regardless, my damned heart beats against me. It feeds blood to this untied pain that leaves its own life. A pain that wakes up before I do and haunts my dreams at night.

This is not because of my son. He was not like this.

Now he sleeps in God's rest, he breaths His smells of hope. I believe him alive as He sees him.

Don't raise your finger, don't ask me reasons for your doubts, you who live painless and faithless. Even if I feel friendly hands grab mine, I don't find them sincere and I let them slide on the ice of the indifference. I catch the white of the sun, the cold of the wind, the darkness of the night. I fall down. No, I actually throw myself to the ground and I hug it. The wheat uprooted months ago is caressing my back while the sky goes down behind the vault of the horizon and the warm afternoon wind is blowing up my chest with sadness.

15

October 2005

(3rd *October, 2005)*

Then life pulled me away abruptly from my legs bent on the tombstone. I should have done it on my own. I used to tell him: "Do not ever run away! Behind your good soul there is a determined man." And yet you passed away with my words on your skin. You used to look at me with that confident expression of who wouldn't have disappointed his father. Instead, you did it. The anger even before the sorrow feeds my tears.

(13th October, 2005)

18

Sometimes his girlfriend comes to see me. I wish she wouldn't do it. This forces me to live her sorrow too and this is too much for me. She would have beautiful eyes if they wouldn't be exhausted by tears and a fresh mouth ready to smile. Her hands are eager for things to seize. They are like new cables looking for bollards in safe harbours. Lately I have waited for her in the afternoons, so I can make a moka and air the rooms. I wait for her to tidy myself up.

(21st October, 2005)

I don't go out willingly, not even to do the shopping. I am forced to walk a long distance to buy some food. I don't work anymore and I have no money. I usually shop in the suburbs where discount supermarkets have the best prices:

- *Tomato sauce □ 0,40*
- *Six bottles of bear □ 1,89*
- *1kg of unbranded pasta □ 0,35*
- *Frozen vegetable soup 1kg □ 1,02.*

I walk among the pallets displayed randomly while I can hear unfamiliar languages spoken. I don't look at anybody. I don't see any colour, I can't smell anything. A woman asks me something, maybe a price too small for her old eyes. My glance is lost beyond her, at the end she gives up.

A soap for my personal hygiene is enough, whereas my beard is celebrating its four months. The coffee is next to the cashier, I will take it at the end. I want a quality brand, but not for me. I go home now. Francesca will come. I want the good smell of coffee to welcome her, to fill the silence of the cold rooms.

We will dispel tears caressing each other cheeks, just a few formal words will put the clock forward.

We do not talk about death. Never! It is already too much around here. To tell the truth, we do not have real conversations. May be one.

We share our dreams...as they were the real life, as they were the only place where to build the future. We are whispering them, frightened they would disappear. This is not difficult to me, this darkness is my home. Such dark muffles every noise, my voice too. With all this dark around, only one thing is easy...waiting. This is the only thing I am still able to do well.

Sometimes I set the house in order. I pick crumbles from the table, I pick the chair fallen from the table together with the curses said while I bite my lips so God does not hear them. I wait until Francesca rings at the door. Today I am happier because she stayed a little longer.

She caressed my beard with such a confidence that I was not expecting between the two of us. I do not know if I want her caresses or not. I am confused, but I let her do it. Her hands were smelling like the sea, as a far away wave. She was talking while caressing my beard. Her hands were moist with emotions, I think. But what am I saying, it can't be possible! I am crazy! Which emotion? I could be her father. If Paolo were alive I would see them playing and laughing for no reasons. A sun that lifts its rays from the earth to the sky.

Without him she is like a beautiful butterfly regressed into a pupa. Who knows! Soon she will find a new sun that will let her fly again. I am sure about this.

November–December 2005

(12ᵗʰ November, 2005)

A Ministry official together with a lieutenant of the Carabinieri came. He has an annoying and fake expression of sadness. A self-controlled gesture limited by his branded shirt. It is not his fault, but I am angry and disgusted.

I blame whoever did not prevent that insane man from killing my son. Now they know who did it and they talk to me about some 'preventive measures' and indemnity. I do not care. I ask about his family instead.

They know little. They leave after other useless reassurances, yet an irksome feeling is telling me they will be back. I do not know why I was so biting with them, maybe I do not want any stranger close to my deep sorrow. Meantime, they will send me some money, a kind of down payment. I would not accept it but I have to pay my creditors. Now that I am not working any more, I have debts with good people that I will pay with this coming money. May they take it all. They have to leave me only the coffee for Francesca.

I am upset by this visit. My son has been exhumed for my new sorrow. I prepare a warm bath. I don't need it but I want to melt my new tears in some hot water.

I look at the world from the full bath, all noises are toned down.

I am calm now.

This is like a light hypnosis, a sweet torpor, the veil of the fog, the limbo. I remain here, motionless...

24

(1st December, 2005)

I spend my time waiting for Francesca.

I still hear her shrill voice bouncing on things like rain drops. I see each ray of sun caught by her big black eyes. One short moment of happiness, an involuntary light smile among the floods of my sadness.

Then I wish she would not come any more. All these smiles are an unendurable pain for me. It is five months since my son died. I woke up early this morning, the whole world had a soft and simple night with its uniform dark. Layers of time with no fascination. My wet beard is dropping in front of the mirror. I see my face reflected and the eyes that were laughing while he was telling stories at the table.

Then he hugged me. He used to do that without any shame although he was already a man. Then his goodbye before leaving. He had strong arms and big hands, he used to hug me opening them completely on my back.

I could feel his promise to take care of me when I would get old.

(7ᵗʰ December, 2005)

My electric blue suit is almost two sizes larger.
I do not have another one.
Why should I?
I wear it only for the graveyard. Walking there is such a difficult task. I can't stand the idea the world has lived without my son for so long! I clean the tombstone and I try to pray, but it is impossible here. I hear voices talking behind me, or inside me. They are frenetic and confused. They are screaming my sorrow and I let them do it. I close my eyes and I listen to them. Slowly they turn into a whispered voice, a Gregorian chant of another era. Then suddenly a small hand is holding mine. The voices recede and the sudden silence causes me a dizziness. Francesca is here!

We do not talk, maybe we are waiting for a thin voice from the back of the new tombstone. We set the flowers in order, we clean the grave, we dry the dewdrops from the picture and we hold each other hands.

Thus we are at the exit of the graveyard. I wish she wouldn't leave me. She strongly hugs me and touches my cheeks with her wet ones. I let her do this once again.

Although her hands do not have promises for me, I haven't felt so good since long time. Her kiss is a present sent from Heaven. I am standing holding back new tears while she leaves.

(15th December, 2005)

The name of my son called out in the courtroom is strongly echoing like whiplashes on my naked back.

The judge does not look at me, ever. I should not have come. What could they have done to me? A lawyer with an empty look is quietly defending the supporters of the "legitimate" war against the Western countries. He is trying to change the history of that damned 7th July. I never thought I was so capable of hating.

This is a preliminary meeting and my attorney looks at me at every "strong" message.

I do not like him either.

I leave this stage where my son is the main actor without being able to say a damned word. I am outside waiting on a wood bench, "Listen, I do not want to come here anymore. Do not force me to be present. Follow your conscience and then you will tell me. I have a son to cry!"

I know I convinced him then we will see.

(17th December, 2005)

Today I shaved, just to do something. I look like a happier man without that harsh beard, but I am not. I better go out and see the sunshine. I want to see it rise and set.

"My love, if you could see December's sun. It is wonderful, gentle and huge enough to cover with a ray the whole world. And in the evening it looks even better. It tears up the clouds in pieces and makes them bleed orange shades, never the same colour, never the same picture. It is never the same dream."

I always talk to my son at sunset, I have the feeling that he is there with me at that time. And I tell him I have a project. I want to die when he resuscitates, so we can meet at the death's door. The moment before I forget everything, I would smell his perfume while hugging him. He could speak a word to me, a last message.

One of those words that you say when you are sure that you won't see each other anymore, instead of saying something like: "Hi Pa, prepare some tortellini that I am coming back tonight." This sentence is suspended between the evening and night, something said with distraction looking elsewhere. A speech lost among the noises of the house; words without any value other than to see others added for a lifetime. Damn it!

(20th December, 2005)

Francesca was smiling too much while having her coffee today. Will she have to tell me anything? She was softly blowing the cup and looking at me. She has the usual fresh and mischievous face that Paolo liked so much.

"Are you busy tomorrow?" She knows perfectly that it is more than five months than I haven't done anything. I should not answer with another question but I am not able to say anything else.

"Why?"

"I am not taking a no! I took half a day off to spend together. You have to come."

And her thin index finger that whips the air is an unsuccessful threat.

(21ˢᵗ December, 2005)

We are already in the car. A light scent of green apple makes that narrow space more acceptable. I am putting myself at ease, while Francesca turns the radio on to cover that dreadful silence. And yet I am not so sad today.

I am thinking without attention to lives that fly and this sun hanging in the air while my hands are caressing the wind outside the window. After a long drive we are in the parking of a Mall. I did not even know there was one.

I remembered the Savoia-Marchetti factory with thick windows large as main doors and an untidy grass all around.

This large building is now at its place, it is nameless and it is faking cheerfulness. In front of it, a huge parking has killed every shadow. Everything here seems to be thrown away. Some ragged festoons are whipping the air. This let me think about a recent opening.

Francesca takes me by the arm and brings me to a clothing store. Inside a long raw of clothes looks like an army standing at attention. The woman who is coming forward has a malicious smile under a heavy make-up. She is talking about fashion but I am not listening to her. Francesca shows light smiles trying to match that unnecessary emphasis with my complete indifference.

Then I try on a suit. They say it fits me well.

I feel Francesca's hands touching the cloth. They are little flying swallows. I can feel them deeply.

At the end I decide to buy it, it is the cloth of a caress. I could not leave it there.

(23rd December, 2005)

It is raining incessantly. This winter is shuffling the cards as it reverses the leaves. Dark and intense sky. It makes me feel depressed without looking at it. I haven't seen Francesca. She has been taken away. I think it is better! Then why am I preparing coffee at two to throw it away at three?

I presume it is to spread a good smell over the house. I hope I can see her, after all. I do not give importance to my thoughts.

There is certainly a better destiny for her. A cold wind is blowing among the clefts of the doors. I hold my crossed arms tightly, shaking off the shivers.

(31st December, 2005)

Here is the last day of this dreadful year. A day like all the others. I have no new calendars to replace the old one. A heavy rain washes away this year from the streets, full of undone and unsaid things.

I look at the window that is crying my tears. I haven't shed tears for a long time. Outside the darkness swallows any noise and the noble silence of the night reveals the precious soul of someone who still has hopes to live.

I am leaning against the doorjamb, with my hands in my pockets. I am waiting for midnight and the celebration noises of the New Year.

I stare at the fire flowers rising from the dark sky before I go to bed. As usually, my 15 drops of Minias are rolling up the blankets. Then midnight comes without any emotion. The sky is lightened up by fireworks that last for a sigh. I am standing still to give the impression I am not existing, I don't want to be in that party. A silly way to feel close to my son. Suddenly, something makes me jump. I can feel it before I see it. I am waiting for the night to be lightened up again.

At the bottom, next to the gate, a bundle of wet rags. I look with staring eyes until the firework illuminates it. It is a thin crouched body, trying to hold its warmth. I check better, I can see blond hair.

The psychiatric drug I take leads me to a sort of day-dream. I am not cold, I do not feel the rain that gets me wet while I walk to the gate staring at that body. I take it up and hold it tight in my arms.

I wish it stops shaking.

I feel frail bones creaking under the fast heart bit.

It makes me feel anxious like an electric shock on my skin. Under the lights of my house I recognise Francesca in my arms.

Despite my anger I stay still, there is little I can do, and for the second time in the same year I feel the evanescence of my strength.

I am a whisper in a strong wind, a tear in a rainy day and I curse the life without even knowing who I should be angry with. Then I strongly hug her, my hands are open on her back as promising all my protection. The gesture I would have liked for me. She doesn't talk, she is hiding her face under my chin while sobbing in pieces.

Then she whispers, "I left him, he was a violent man. I do not know where to go. I have you only, don't send me away."

My head is full of words without any form, only lots of lights in the never ending darkness of my soul and I am troubled. It is better not to tell anything! I lay her down on the sofa. A blanket. I go and prepare a warm bath. I am staring at the steam deleting things of this room.

The opaque mirror is reflecting a thin silhouette, almost slender. The skin reddened for the cold tastes like the first fruits. I beckon to her to come forward and I remain seated on the border of the bath.

I watch closely the red stains on her white skin that look like roses inside a glass. Her naked body finally gets some colour in the hot water. She is an angel

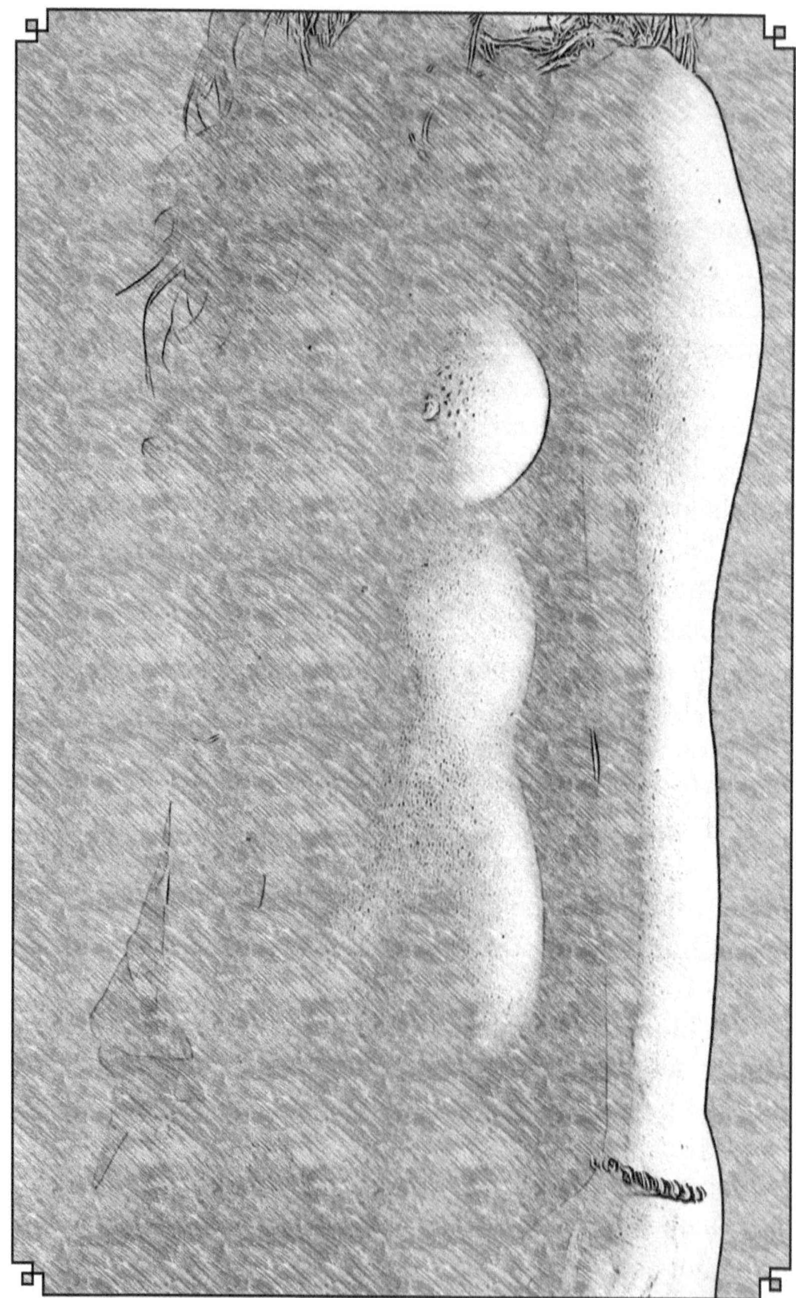

resting on a cloud. She has a small breast, very light nipples.

Her hands move in the surface of the water blending her body lines and I am confused between what I "should" and what I "would like".

I am flying over the sky, on top on everything. I dip my arms into the water until I touch her warm body. Her rose into my hand opens its petals. I lost my identity... I lost my memory!

Her kisses move through the nerves of my neck, I feel as the life of my son is flowing in me again. I can't taste anything, I only see perspectives as if it was a movie. Paolo's eyes shine in mine. I am grazing her with his hands, like the wind with ears of corn. I don't look at Francesca however I feel her soft skin like sand that stopped shaking...yet throbbing. I am lost, her young body is pressing against mine; the silk pajamas get wet but my morality tells me not to take it off.

Francesca is well determined! I would like to see her confused.

I would like to be called "Paolo..."

I remain like this for an endless time, the complete tour of the sun around the universe. The perfect time that she calls me with my son name. Here the magic... now he is alive. I can let myself go. He lives again and I do not exist anymore.

I hear the echo of his heart bit hitting my chest, shaking it among the ribs. I kiss her sweetly and I keep on doing it all the night. We fall asleep in a hug, exhausted after forcing us to be something else, someone else, completely wet of water and humours...

January 2006

(1ˢᵗ *January, 2006*)

It's late in the morning when an expected fever wakes me up. I feel my eyes burning in their sockets and the cold makes me shake.

I am alone and tired but I am sure it was not a dream.

I lay under the blanket for an entire day.

In the dark my eyes are shimmering small flames of fever, I am upset and I have a bad headache. I have the taste of the night on my dried lips. I remain like this, still and exhausted for other two days while the high fever plays weird effects.

I can hear a beautiful music. A sweet melody as soft as a mother's caress. Sometimes the doorbell rings stressfully. Nothing will make me get up to check who is at the door. Then nothing more. Only music, music like on the sea's waves, like on the dune's lines. My head is on fire, my throat is dry but I don't move from the bed. My neck is stiff like a pole buried forcefully, only that music relieves me. I wouldn't mind dying like this. I stay still, waiting to choke in my own sighs.

(4th January, 2006)

The clock cuts time in thin slices; razor blades. The night stretches on my bleeding wounds. Finally, I am dying. I have desired it so much. The pain I had in the past few days, although annoying, was a new sensation. The fever. The warm wind of Scheol. I will wait for the night. Dying in the silence of the darkness is less brutal.

(11th January, 2006)

I had hoped for a whole week, but my body won at the end. I am hungry. I don't think I will die this time. My muscles don't ache anymore. I feel well rested and strong. Even the music has gone, I feel again the sad and cold silence as before. I turn on the stereo after a long time and I listen to a record of Engelbert Humperding. The telephone is ringing endlessly, I finally answer but somebody is speaking in English. I don't know what he is saying, I can understand very little English and I speak it even less, however when he finished what I believe it is a question, by instinct I reply "yes". Silence once again, then I hear Lucia's voice. She is not talking, she calls out my name while sobbing. I hadn't heard from her for five years.

My heart is bleeding on my chest, my desolation is a gush of blood coming out. I am speechless. She knows it, I am sure. Our son has died. I was not able to protect him and I feel so guilty in front of her too.

"Where are you?" I am trying to let her talk.

"In Australia. I couldn't call you earlier, I was in the middle of nowhere. Wait for me, I am looking for a flight to come home."

Home? Which home! She has never had one, but I do not have any resentment. I know her sorrow is even deeper than mine.

"What are you going to do?" she yells at me.

"About what...?" I reply with surprise.

"I am talking about our son's murderers. We have

to decide how to face them. But you, how are you?"

I would like to tell her I am already dead, but this doesn't have any sense. I do not know what else to add.

"What can I say, Paolo is no longer with us. I can't bear the weight of his absence."

I recall her sentences. I didn't realise what she said. What does she expect me to do! This phone call has upset me, it has agitated me. How could I revenge my son.

"I will wait for you, then we'll decide...take care."

"I will let you know when I am back, but I do not think I will be able to return earlier than three weeks. See you soon."

Her free and strong spirit, her distance from everything hurts me. My sorrow is alive again, I need to do something. I go out.

My red roses need care. I wear my gloves and I trim them. Their thorns catch my sweater, I turn to see who is pulling me. It is so weird, it seems as they want to comfort my tears. While trimming, I recall the time I met Lucia. I feel the same emotion, I feel my heartbeat on my temples. It is some fresh nourishment for my memories; an alive thought. So much alive that I see her materialised. I shrug my shoulders trying to get rid of my bad mood. Melancholy is like a coloured glass that filters the light. Lonely tears taste stale and make you feel better when you lose them. Everything goes too fast for my senses.

Then to track my course I hold my life with two fingers and taste it, smoothly rubbing it as you do with a good olive oil.

I find myself twenty-two years younger.

A cold morning in March, I was fastened in my heavy coat while looking outside the window, waiting for my barley coffee to boil.

"Should I go out in this weather?" I was asking myself. Though the real questions was, "Do I want to see it happen?"

I told her to meet me in front of Café Zoppi's along the church's street. The leaves were whirling in the air, mixing perspectives and ideas. At the same speed of the wind my thoughts were tangling fears with good intentions, but at this point, it was worth...

I met Lucia at a chess class. Teachers told members to get in contact also by letter. I had not met her in person yet. She had an almost hermaphrodite nickname and immediately I had the feeling she was a strong man. She didn't correct me when I addressed her as she was a male. Maybe she wanted to let me believe she was. Then she got mistaken and I immediately caught it. I naturally started to talk as a man to a woman. I was courting her discretely and she seemed to like it, adding many smiling emoticons as answers to my compliments.

We used to play intense games, I was pragmatic and she was unpredictable. She knew how to move the "knight" very well. At every game, I got an idea about her. She couldn't bear to be under pressure, she was disposed to lose important pieces to get rid of it. Suddenly, one day I throw out a sentence: "I want to kiss you!" An island of words in a sea of silence. "Damn, why did I say it..."

That phrase came from nowhere, it was neither said by my heart nor by my tongue burning with passion. So what?

Maybe I was just sounding on Lucia's skin. At least I would have tested the consistence of her NO! She waited before answering. I imagined her tasting the words against her palate, as they were a good "red" wine.

She was a woman, not a girl, she wouldn't have done anything thoughtless. She wouldn't have moved by such an ordinary sentence and I knew I hadn't been original.

However, now I have an advantage, I am waiting for an answer. "Yes" or "No", a clean sound among her teeth, a gust of wind firmer than the others.

"...You are too impetuous. I wouldn't have said that from your way of playing. If you were here, you would see my embarrassment."

How much predictable we are when courting! Nobody has ever complained about this. Now I was sure! She liked me and I was ready to take her into a more intimate level of the game.

"Where would you like I give you my first kiss?" Once again, I throw out a sentence.

"You'll see when you will want to meet me. I have more fire than my flame can tell...my dear." Here she is, unveiled. Words are losing thickness and colour now. Looking for new ones could spoil the wait. When the magician discloses his trick, the stage loses its magic. I do not know what else to say, those words thrilled among the fingers and on the pen, hidden among the buttons of the typewriter, do not count any more. I look for an appropriate place for a date, I would like her to be at her ease.

Along the tree-lined street there is a café full of mirrors and warm colours.

"I will meet you on Wednesday, the 9th March at the café Zoppi's. I will be there at 9pm. I hope you'll come…"

I thought I would weaken my emotions giving her an appointment ten days later. That 9th March in 1983 was as "inflated" of wind as the night before.

All that air seemed to unveil new transparent views under a pale sky, still uncertain if turning lighter or darker. Then the evening finally came.

She is wrapped in a short goose dawn, tight at the waist. She has long wavy hair, unleashed on purpose. It would not be comfortable with such a windy day. Her dark eyes look like some October afternoons, they have the same colour of the sand in the shadow of the dunes, they smile on their own before her lips.

Her small resting glasses keep her thoughts away from curious people. What a masterpiece is her mouth! It is perfectly proportionate with round tips and a vermilion colour that gets lighter every time she bites her lips; I am eager for those silky lips.

We share a friendly greeting and the round table of the café is the right distance for two who meet for the first time. The large glass windows show the branches of the trees shaken by the wind like a silent movie.

I glance outside to gain time. As soon as the green tea is served, she holds the cup in her hands blowing over it. She is stunning behind the veil of steam and I try hard to say the right words to fascinate her. Her bright eyes are like stretched strings on my race. I did not think I could feel so hampered. The conversation is centred in the dreary weather and work. I give a glance at the titles of the newspaper on the table next to us... "Reagan announces the space shield" I read it quickly.

Finally, Lucia looks at me straight into my eyes: "You are very nice, I am lucky."

"Wow! Do you really think it?! Never as much as you are..." I whisper while I get close to kiss her.

Now our eyes search each other with a new glow, perhaps the light of anger for the wasted words in that café spread to cover space and time.

It is late: "Taxi...taxi..." and she left already. Maybe she has never been here!

The night has come with its shadows and a new annoying gloominess. I stare at the empty space, sighing with noise.

The TV talks on its own. I look at the news without paying attention, Borg is retiring and I envy him, he is so measured and elegant whereas I am walking in my house in great distress. I have been always sure I would have never said "I love you" to a woman. Perhaps to a son but never to a woman. And now instead, victim of a vertigo, I have lots of small "I love you" to whisper. I need to get rid of this load. No more words weighted within the limit of "good manners"! I call and invite her at my house for the following night. I would have welcomed her skin smelling like chestnuts.

As she enters, she takes off her coat as a petal falling from a rose. (I am anxious like an acrobat on the rope.)

Her hands point at things that she likes with shimmering eyes. I think the room is full of light and butterflies.

I revere her. Desiring her so ardently is a sacrilege that I commit with an embarrassing arrogance. Our humours blend on top of our lips, her arms are on my neck and mine on her hips.

Then I do not remember anything else.

I only recall her round breast on my naked chest. I was in heaven. I had searched this in other lips, in other women, and now satisfied with unknown whispers, I found it in that velvet body tight to mine. She did not have defects.

Perfect was her smell, her mouth, her body, the moment...

Since that day, a full year of happiness has gone. I immediately gave her the keys of my house. She couldn't come often, but the idea I would have found her at home in the evening was making the day sweet. Sometimes she was naked and audacious. I opened the door and found her in front ready to make love. Other times she prepared dinner. Then I could smell the good food from the stairs. She liked surprising me, being unpredictable.

I welcomed her like the colour I was missing.

"What a nice couple we are," I used to say. Then, a night of a day without history, I came home late. I found her in the dark of the living room.

I distinguished the borders of the objects as close as I walked to her, sat on the sofa with the light off, led by her chocked sobs. I imagined her bad mood, she would send me away with her whimpers.

I was able to cancel her pout with my caresses. Not this time. She was carrying the problem, a new life was about to certify how much we loved.

That's what I thought. She did not. She was waiting for her anthropologist colleagues to contact her for a job in Papua New Guinea and she could not accept it with a son to grow.

I was searching for some points of reference in the dark, I needed to reflect before talking.

I was looking at her with a different light. I could not recognise her, but I still loved her.

"It will not be a problem, I will take care of the baby. I will be a mother too." I desired that so much. That is how she could live her "life in every continent". She used to call often. She always sent letters and presents, the classic way to appease the conscience. We forgave her.

After a while, my existence with Paolo was stable and our relation so deep that we could not think about a different life. Amen!

Now the destiny has shuffled the cards. While I take a shower to wash the sweat fever, I wonder what I should do of my broken life. I am confused between the kisses of a girl I do not love and who will never bring my son back and the words of the only woman I have ever loved.

Motionless, under the warm water, I am waiting for an inspiration, a word coming from my stomach like a gushing back, a shiver.

Anything that would give me the strength to live or to die.

(22nd January, 2006)

After three full weeks I see Francesca again, she is waiting for the door to open. I see her distorted through the spy-hole. Her rush annoys me. A silly weakness is evidently the cause of my irritation. I say this now that I have stomach cramps for the remorse of having made love with her. It is not the same anymore. She knows it too.

We were victims of a suggestion, we thought it could have given us Paolo back. I take the greatest blame, having dirtied that nice face smiling at me behind the smokes of a coffee. Why is she here? I was sure that leaving in a rush without greeting meant to disappear. I wait a little more. She is less charming with that insistent ring. We remain at the door looking each other, our thoughts crowd willing to get out quickly. This silence is strong like a violent slap. I let her in; once inside her look gets sweeter: "Will you prepare a coffee?" and she takes off her coat. Does she think nothing happened?! I believe she is acting to gain some time. I let her do it.

I prepare the coffee, I get changed. I see her pouring it into the cups. She tries to engage in a conversation. "Do you remember Maria, she was your neighbour and her husband was in my office..."

I interrupt her. I look outside the window. "You know that it will not happen again, right? It was foolish, Paolo will not come back."

Her answer is unexpected.

"You cannot leave me in this way, I lost your son and now I am also loosing you."

I see her in a new light. A woman who has reasons to argue. However, this is just a grazed thought.

"You lost him only, I have never been yours. We got involved in an alchemy to get Paolo back for one night. If it ever happens again, it would be a different thing."

I say this suffocating my anger, but I am very firm in telling these words and finally we cry together.

My cold coffee is like a small lake in the night. I dip my eyes in hoping to find new words to convince her to leave, but she stays in front of me crying. I take her coat and I pull it on her shoulders, while the coffee I throw in the earth of the geraniums is the right metaphor for the impossible love between us. I see her leaving.

I know she will have to lick her wounds before giving up to the strength of a new hug, but it will be inevitably like this.

March 2006

52

(16th March, 2006)

Two more months have gone by. It has been a languid and heavy time like melted lead. The company of my broken TV and some shadows spread all over make my mood bad.

The slow gestures, my muscles slowed down by medication dilate the time in seconds heavy like light years. I can't bare it anymore!

I am not scared of being consciousness of my son death anymore. I have feared it so much that I am accepting it now. It is like a tumour that dries out the organs inside. I instead feel distressed by meeting Lucia. I was not expecting to be so coward! Her sorrow has dignity, hold by her hands on her hips, her lips bitten not to cry. I could not stand it. I fear her resolute words, her questions on my careless idleness.

I have dreamed her for some time. She has a wide open mouth screaming at me that I have to revenge the death of our son. A nightmare shacking my skin like a sledge-hammer on iron. But I don't know what to do. I do not have any idea where to start. I do not know where I should go. After the death of that young boy mistaken for a terrorist, I even turned off the radio , shocked by the number of sons the violence is able to generate.

I wish the end of the world...

(20th March, 2006)

I don't have to wait anymore. I'll find the courage to leave! It will be the solution for my useless life, perhaps the extreme sacrifice to make my life less empty now that you are not here anymore. First of all, I need lucidity. I throw my medicines away melting them in water. I look at them reduced to a coloured pulp and I prepare myself to fight against sorrow without barriers. I resist, but I risk to drown in sobs and tears. I have pain in the jaw to tighten my anguish.

55

April 2006

rchi Gates ↑

(3rd April, 2006)

I am getting ready to leave! I heard that Lucia came back a few days ago. She knows my embarrassment and she waits for my clear action before facing me. I am so grateful to her! My heart breaks in my throat. It beats so loudly that I think the station ticket clerk can hear it. I am sure she can. It has been years since I've taken a train and the panorama that speeds outside the window hurts my eyes. Even coming out of the house was a challenge. I felt as if the bright sky could have fallen on my head at any moment...what a heavy feeling.

To tell the truth I ran away!

I am like a mouse when its den is discovered. I am shameful. Darkness and pity were keeping me safe. I will have to reflect on this. The fear that Lucia would have put me in front of her reasons and I could only have answered with my indolence made me run away. This is why I am on this train to Rome. I will understand what to do on the way.

Rome is a city of lost souls as I am. People are walking fast following their thoughts. I am at ease, after all, here or in the darkness of my home I feel the same. The station is a greenhouse protecting me from the spring sun and wind. However, I can't stay long. I can't find the answers to my questions here.

"Taxi...taxi... Are you free? Please, to the Farnesina."

I show my ID and the guard standing at the entrance takes me to the officer who came over to my house. He has a different attitude now. He seems to understand my hesitation, he grabs me by the arm pointing out to a chair. He didn't need to lie. All formal condolences had already been dispatched.

I am looking for confidential information and he, knowing that, would talk about it shortly. His eyes dull of smoke staring at me are about to burst out. His strong tobacco breath bothers me, however I let him whisper what he has to say. When we leave each other outside it's late at night.

Now I have names and addresses, I do not know what to do with them yet. I trust my new instinct, sooner or later I will have a plan. I leave his office with a paper on my hand, to keep up appearances, some information copied from *Il Messaggero* to fill that blank sheet, to justify my signature on the visitors register. The handwritten paper instead has living letters that move by themselves.

I read some Arab names and addresses of English streets. I see their lives while I am horrified for my mere thoughts; I imagine their smiling faces, pleased for the torn lives. I need to get out of bed, my heart has slackened its reins. I am chocking in an anonymous hotel room. I will take a shower and go to bed again. Every hour is like a club striking on Paolo's tombstone, I see his bones shaking under those strokes.

My sleep is troubled. It is like an earthquake for my soul. I already know that I will survive... I already know what I will do tomorrow.

(5ᵗʰ April, 2006)

It is early morning. I read the newspaper about Gene Pitney's death. I do not care anymore about others death, neither the one of the singers I loved in my youth. This spring morning smells nothing and I strongly breath this insipid air. I try to raise my head, but the sky is still too bright for my eyes. Things are better like that. I will look downward. Today I feel a different man. I have no idea if I will find my enemies smiling or satisfied. I do not care. I will make sure they are not.

"Fiumicino, here we are," says the taxi driver.

Even the last flight to London has already left. I will have to wait, but I am not going to go back to the city.

I spend the night in the half-dark protection.

Every now and then a voice calls out passengers to the gate. I fall asleep. I dream. I see a sky that does not hurt me, I am happy without a real reason. I lifted my feet from the ground and I fly over towns and fields. I follow the sunlight but I don't go to London, I believe it is the direction to join my son. That's why I am happy.

I wish to continue to sleep even when my plane is announced in the morning. This is my first flight. Only now I realise it. I climb the plane's stairs fast, to conceal my fear. It is very exciting instead. From up here the sky is less scary, I feel closer to God who is guarding my son. But I immediately dismiss this thought. I have evil plans, I do not want the presence of God over me; I am like a rabid dog dressed in black.

I do not have plans. I only want to add one more link to the chain of hate.

Here is London, finally. Here the atmosphere is surreal. In the morning a cotton wool of fog muffles the sun's sparkle; there is a burning smell... I can hear bombs ready to explode again.

(7th April, 2006)

Three days later I haven't any idea of what to do yet. I went to Edgware Road tube station. My son died here.

I heard the explosion, the screams, the moans and I couldn't stand it. I ran far away. I ran until my muscles could take it. I am not so strong after all. I carry on walking following the acrid smell of spices. The Indian quarter is a sad village swallowed in a big city. The houses are corners of grey bricks, inside hostile looks weave wanted canvas. Nobody likes to come here and I stay only as long as I need to. I am looking for a small handy revolver.

That was easy, I only had to ask the guy that was looking at me from the other side of the street.

"Come back here in three days."

After an "OK!" we have nothing else to say.

(10th April, 2006)

I feel alone! I miss the sea! I didn't go there often but I could feel it; it was a way out. The direction of sailing souls swollen by a good wind. I was homesick for my "emerald green" sea, stories told by a father to a son. I am not saying it was the best sea in the world. Actually, the stones beach was so uncomfortable to keep people away, making the sea even more mine and Paolo's. Already in spring, we used to spend full afternoons there. They were the best.

We stole those hours from the day, we forced ourselves, now I understand why. They are the balm to massage on my skin, they calm down my shivers while I ask questions dangerous for my safety. It is an exaggerated fear, at the end it is even too easy. Nobody cares about you. Show money and you can ask whatever you want.

Three days later, I have a Beretta "tomcat3032" in my pocket. It is shiny grey. The filthy fellow that gave it to me was proud of having stolen it from a gang leader. He was boasting of his name. I pretended to be surprised recognising that name.

In reality, I feel taken into this situation by force and reaching the bottom will be an operation of titanic proportions for me.

63

May 2006

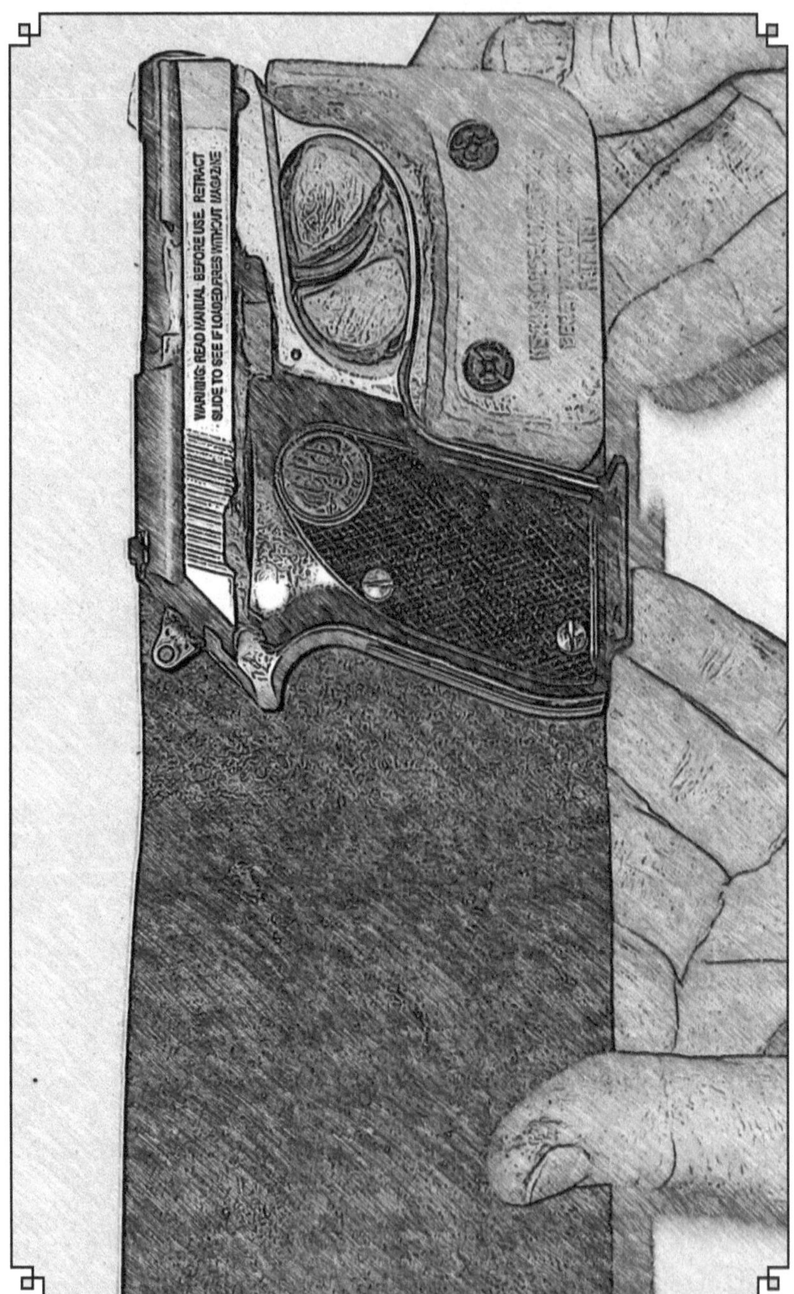
WARNING: READ MANUAL BEFORE USE. RETRACT SLIDE TO SEE IF LOADED. FIRES WITHOUT MAGAZINE

(4th May, 2006)

65

I would like to be buried in the shadow of my empty house. I would like to stay still for the eternity, hanging and fainting under the hits of the time that goes by. I am here instead. I test my courage or rather my recklessness while I walk around the London quarters with the gun hidden in my pocket. It is like a detached appendix! It lives its own life, it snarls at every suspect pedestrian like a wild animal longing for bites. It takes my breath away. I am exhausted by the anger shaking from my feet without knowing what to do with that.

(10th May, 2006)

"I am looking for a job to be able to stay in London for a few months, can you help me?"

Once I learnt this sentence, I knock at every small shop in Allington Road where I found a room to rent. I thought it was a good idea to start from shops with "Vera Pizza" signs. But the oriental faces that I see inside look like a fraud.

At the third attempt, I found a job; at least they have an Italian with them now. In the afternoon, I have already a cap with "La Vera Pizza" on it.

Golden red jacket, I am ready for home delivering. I wasn't expecting to be the delivery "boy" at fifty years old but they do not want me steady in the shop – I understand them – I would be the only real piece in a pack of fake cards. The owner is Chinese, not even too much Oriental. He speaks perfect English and luckily he is as indolent and friendly as a good Neapolitan.

It's all for the best.

(15th May, 2006)

I follow directions on the London's map. These unknown streets keep me focused on deliveries.

I am not bothered in wearing this funny jacket that makes me look like a tamed monkey. This is enough to explain my little interest in life.

Every morning I walk through the entrance of Edgware Road tube, its sign is still black of smoke as if wounded. Stairs go down to the darkness. An open mouth screaming out for the deep sorrow of those dead. My sorrow! It is a silent shout, choked at the first note, as it happens to whoever does not find solution to his anger. My son was dying when he was carried away from here.

I have no reasons to forgive myself.

I spit on the ground, the bitter taste of disgust.

↑ Platforms 2, 3

69

June 2006

(3rd June, 2006)

I am getting accustomed to this place! The funny jacket makes me odd but not dangerous, nobody cares about me unless he has ordered a pizza. "You pay it only if you get it in half an hour."

This is the policy of the company; mine too if I want my wage. And now, I am the best. I have nothing else to do, I can stay after my regular working hours and I can go further than my three districts I usually serve in the "city". However, I do not work in the evening.

I feel the burden of my fifty years, above all when the night falls. My eyes are weak. Darkness confuses everything, the roads on the map, the street signs. This is an excuse. At night London gets quieter and I move better in the obscurity. I try to understand, I ask questions, I follow persons. Newspapers still write about the investigation on terrorists. I collect press-cuttings. The ministry's offices suggested me to keep in touch with them, but I will not. I do not want anyone on my trajectory.

(6th June, 2006)

There is a faded sky over the English countryside. Little raindrops trace unknown routes. The dull green of the fields looks like struck by God's sadness. But I don't care. I am going to a precise place. There are rumours of searches in the North area of Dwesbury. It's the district where Mohammed Sadique Khan lived, the terrorist who killed my son and before that…a father and a special needs teaching assistant. Damn what dizziness is life! Discern and insanity get mixed in a bustle hiding the straight line to the precipices. I get off the bus resolutely, I want to anticipate my thought. I don't have to give it the time to hold me back.

There is a beautiful residential quarter in front of me. I am amazed. The trimmed grass is perfect. White stones are nicely displayed along the borders to indicate pedestrian paths. Clusters of cream coloured small detached houses look the same in shape and size. Everywhere the scenery is identical.

The white doors have frosted glass portholes. I can imagine the life in those houses even without seeing it. A yellow, warm light goes through the windows' glass in the slight dark of the late afternoon. Busy people cross the rooms, I can tell from the light switched off as if the main door closes its only eye, winking. What a strange calm. The air has a light red shade, maybe a dying sunbeam painted it; the last one that hits the Earth.

No one is walking in this surreal atmosphere. Now

the soft brown grass and the ocher houses look like an abandoned movie set. I don't feel like going anywhere. I feel like a still figure in a picture, a brush stroke inside a smooth frame.

Suddenly, a car arrives. It comes slowly and silently. It is an old Mercedes, one of those with the chrome radiator on display. It swerves from the main street to a porphyry driveway that ends in a garage. The bronze numbers on the door and on the garage match. I have no doubts anymore about who they are. The four passengers are not in the rush to get off. I can't distinguish in the obscurity, however more than once I have the impression that they turn to my side.

Then, they get off. They quickly walk home without looking at me. They pretend not to be curious on purpose. Certainly, this plan was agreed while in the car. The oldest is standing at the door letting the others in first, while staring at me. There, under the lights, I see his Middle Eastern origin and some sprinkle of snow on his dark and crispy hair. Soon after the door closes, the bright glow slit disappears.

This gentle darkness of the night is perfect again. I must be crazy! The bus to London is leaving in fifteen minutes and I am walking towards that door. I can't believe what I am going to do! My finger is firmly pointing to the doorbell. I won't say a word, I only want they see me, they know. The door slowly opens, they know already I am out there. I am facing the oldest man I just saw a few minutes ago. He has a dark round face.

I am so close to him that I see his lost serenity in the eyes. He doesn't talk to me, my intentions are completely disarmed, I keep my arms down and I stare at him.

"Look at me. I lost my son because of you, now you have a real enemy to fight, not just an idea." I think it but I don't say it.

I am not going to say this to this men who I feel so close to me, as if his destiny was accomplished, like mine after all. Then a few little quick footsteps and here comes a chubby baby, badly dressed, yet beautiful with his peaceful look. He moves close to the leg of the old man who holds his head to protect him. My face can not avoid hurting with a smile…it is the first one after a long time. I don't notice the young man who meanwhile, approached the door, looks at my funny jacket underneath the raincoat. "We didn't order anything, try to ring to our neighbour's door. He usually orders your pizzas."

He gently moves the old man's hand away and slowly closes the door to my face, without any rush. I don't know how long I stand there. Then I turn and walk to the bus station in the deep darkness. The waiting-room is empty and sloppy. I hear odd echoes inside this place. Frogs are croaking tirelessness to the moon in the fields far away. I hear a metallic noise. I hear footsteps walking towards me. My fear is like a blade on my stomach.

Luckily, the bus with the illuminated sign "London City" arrives. It stops puffing air from the brakes. I get in as fast as I can, while two shadows dissolve in the obscurity.

It is a full night travel and I recall my experience

looking for a reason of revenge. Leicester…here are the first houses of London. The city has just woken up. I have only the time to change my wet clothes and lay my gun down. I look myself in the mirror in search of an alchemy that makes me wiser and more determined.

July 2006

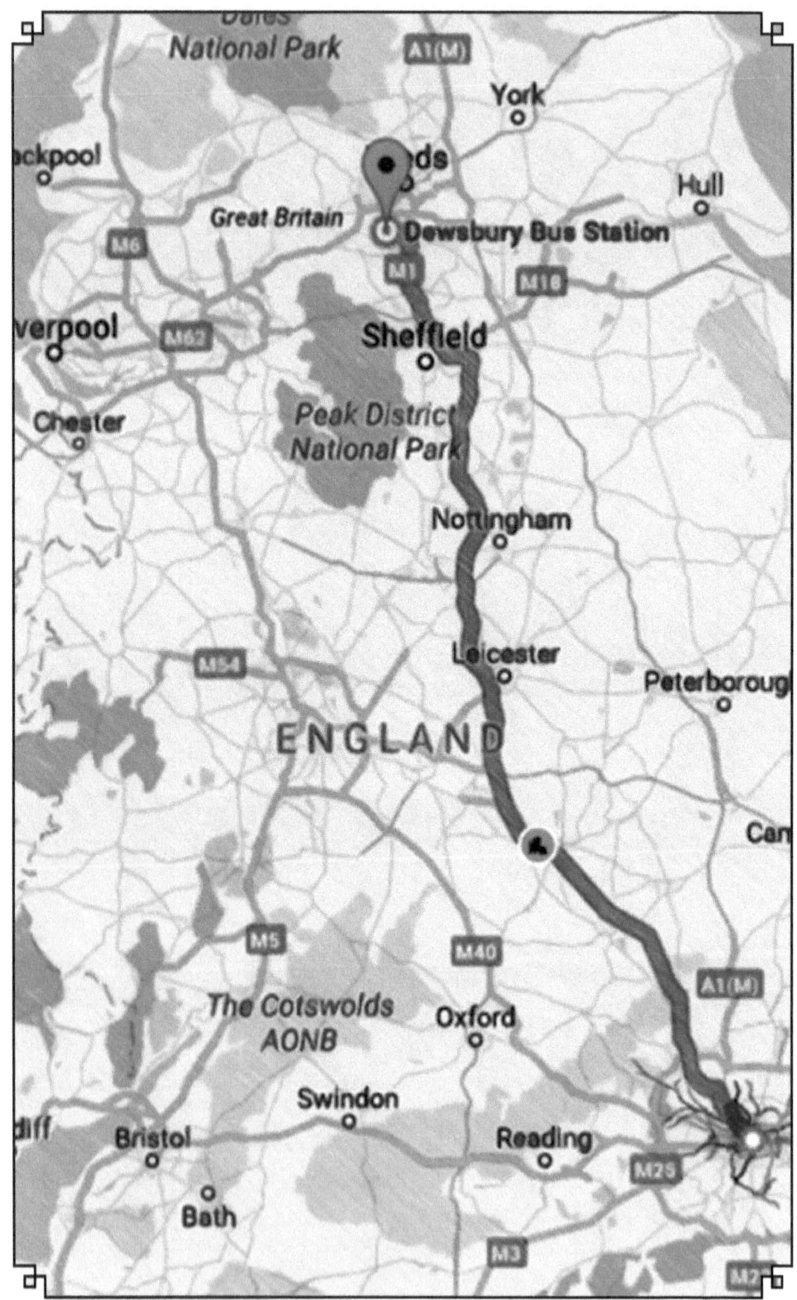
Dales
National Park
A1(M)
York
Blackpool
Hull
Great Britain
ds
Dewsbury Bus Station
M6
M1
M18
Liverpool
M62
Sheffield
Chester
Peak District
National Park
Nottingham
Leicester
M54
Peterborough
ENGLAND
Can
M5
M40
The Cotswolds
AONB
Oxford
A1(M)
Swindon
diff
Bristol
Reading
M25
Bath
M3
M2

(7th July, 2006)

It's been a year since Paolo died! I can't think about it! The death of a son is not an anniversary. Since then, every day, he has gone in the mornings and resuscitated in my dreams at night. Today I will not do anything different than usual. My sadness is screaming so loud that makes my ears bleed. Dazed, I go to work. The day passes slowly like a funeral cortège. Nothing in this world can move time faster. Nothing can stop me from sighing. It's finally evening and I get drunk for the first time in my life. Sitting at the counter of a pub, I swallow liqueur without counting the shots. There are no mirrors around so I don't see the worst of me. I get out late in the night. I walk in the street without any dignity, urinating in my trousers and in the corners of the houses. At the end, I vomit everything. Only then, the sadness disappears. It remains the bad taste in my mouth. I spit some blood and small fragments of my crystal heart.

(12ᵗʰ July, 2006)

Days go by fast despite my ridiculous golden jacket. Pizzas are delivered on time. I am free in the afternoons, but it is not good that I always come here, in Edgware Road. I sit on the same step – the first – waiting to be swallowed up by the monster. It happened to my son after all, it could happen to me as well. The light of this hour shines upon the first steps…underneath, thousands of people get on the underground trains. I have lived thousands of years unsteady on the first step of a tube station. Every time my skin is torn into pieces, though I "survive" in the armour of my golden red jacket. This is ridiculous!

I haven't heard of Lucia lately. Inside me, instead, I hear her screaming and pushing me, and I caress her dirty hair after the long trip. "Tomorrow I am going to kill them all, don't worry."

I am hanging around instead, dazed by my good nature that fights me as I am the enemy. I will try it again!

I have another ticket to Dwesbury in my pocket. I leave when the fog hides London. Smooth curves drive the bus to Leicester, then Nottingham, Sheffield, and finally Dwesbury. When I arrive the city is already up.

Everybody was shocked knowing that a kamikaze lodged here. In such a respectful place, the gesture of greeting each other at the other side of the street must be the only reason to raise a hand above the head. Not to brandish a gun.

I imagine the murderous hands that killed my son

while caressing the heads of his students a few days before the explosion. I think about this while I am looking at the young woman with a gentle and shy look who is crossing the street. She could be his wife.

Maybe she will accept to talk: "Hasina, Hasina…" I am near her, her expression is disturbed by insanity. Tears left evident traces on her perfect cheeks. I feel tenderness, but I am not control my actions anymore. I try to catch her, I want to talk to her. She is frightened to death. I am not! I walk slowly towards her holding the shopping bag she left in her rush. I am still far when two men get in the middle. She is standing at the door while looking at me. Nobody talks, they look threatening. If they were protected by darkness, they would jump over me, I am sure about this. I drop the bag, I take Paolo's picture from my pocket. He is the only one among us who has a serene expression. This does not help me. I scream all the anger I have in my body. "Somebody has to pay for this…damn you!" and I point at the face in the picture. I don't see the punch coming from the side. It is a rapid one, he must know how to land them. I fall down.

I do not faint and my hand is already on the gun. Lucid, I wait a little before pulling it out. I hesitate, they don't. One stroke and the door closes loudly. Blood is bleeding from the cut on my swollen cheek.

I remain still…my hand in my pocket contains the desire to shoot at those windows to blind the house lodging my enemies. Now I know better my target. The cut is hurting and the blood feeds my resentment, my nerves are on the edge and make me shiver.

(15th July, 2006)

In the following days my job is a balm for my spirit.

I smile while delivering pizzas. I play the fool. The scar has almost disappeared and my soul has recovered faster than my body healing as if by magic, but the impression of being followed makes me anxious, and I often turn back.

"Come on! I have some work to do," I say loud. The Chinese owner trusts me and he lets me do. I have the feeling he thinks I am dangerous, but this is just an idea. How could I be with this funny jacket on.

(29th July, 2006)

I have spent the following two weeks in unaware serenity. Then it happens inevitably... It is a warm night like a formal kiss, a little dark as it is in cities. I go back home after my usual beer on Fridays breathing the late evening air with delight. I knew I was taking a risk. In fact, I wasn't surprised when I got the first blow. Punches seem coming from the night like mighty flapping wings. They appear anywhere from the darkness. The wickedness floating in the air hurls at me. I do not react to the blows. I can't, I wouldn't know what to do. I try to parry them, but they are so strong to erase full days from my calendar.

I throw myself on the ground pretending to faint, maybe they will stop hitting me. It doesn't happen. Slowly, I don't feel pain and I have no more anger to spare.

A kick makes me turn towards the sky. I look at the stars and see them go out one by one over the border of the roofs. I cry (but it might be joy) while the punches become less intense. I hear them tired, snort, spit on me.

One of them leans on me, he whispers in my ears, but the hits on the head have made me deaf. Anyway, I wouldn't understand their language. Now that he is so close I could punch him but I change my mind. I am only willing to limit the damages. Suddenly a scream...and the darkness seems no longer to protect my aggressors. They stand still smelling at the air like wild beasts, then they disappear running away along the walls, where the obscurity does not allow my eyes to follow them. I hear steps fading away quickly, and they continue to hit me with words from the distance. Finally no more blows. I feel no pain, but I am exhausted. I do not care about my dignity, my saliva mixed with blood, the urine lost for fear, my ragged and dirty clothes. I would like to get up, but my muscles are not helping, while I wait for that figure coming toward me.

"Francesca…?!"

She leans on me holding up my head while she gently cleans my swollen face. My soul in rags leaves a disgusting taste in my mouth.

"Look what they've done…bastards!"

"Francesca forget it, it's too dangerous, you shouldn't have come, you have to go now."

"I met Lucia and we talked for a while. She asked me to come. She is worried about you, she doesn't want you put yourself in danger, she waits for you at home. She begged me to bring you back safe and sound and I almost couldn't do it." She firmly insists fully aware of her advantage, she is right.

"I want my revenge first," I reply filled with anger.

She looks at me but she doesn't recognise me. She is not wrong. What am I doing in London beaten to blood with a revolver on my pocket? With Francesca holding me, I reach my hotel. The harsh look of the old doorman is the last "bitter" I have to swallow. I let him think what he wants! Finally, the bed, every single cell of my body is begging for some rest. In the silence of the night, I hear my bones going back to their place. Francesca sleeps on the sofa. I am quiet. I cry in silence, I regret having been so foolish and I collect all my strength with whispers and hate. Tomorrow I will give a final meaning to my being here! I went over my break point.

After the anguish for Paolo's death, this damned fear is the strongest feeling of my balanced life. I have to sit down. I am about to faint. My heart overflows, my breath is short in my chest.

(30th *July, 2006*)

The morning arrives, I am already awake. It is not a good day the one that sees a killer planning murders. This is why I am not smiling either to the sun or to Francesca in her reassuring look. We get ready in silence.

I look at myself in the mirror, my swollen face has changed my features. I don't mind, somebody else will be guilty.

At the bus station people are absent-minded. They irritate me.

What I am doing is for them too. How could they have forgotten the bombs? Only the ticket clerk recognises and greets me. The tiresome trip goes through the same views, without colour or design. Francesca tries to catch my attention. She keeps on talking but her words bounce on my indifference. I don't care for what she has to say. She understands that and puts her hand on my leg.

"I am with you until the end, I just want you to know it."

I do not reply. I think about Lucia, without her push I wouldn't have gone so far. Now she would like to stop me.

The indolence of my rage may not be enough to fulfil my task. – I must remain focused. – I have come up here, I can't consider anything different than revenge, especially after last night. They were strangers. They killed my son and hit me. I don't want them to go beyond. I swallow time and street as a shark. I will not allow any more thoughts between myself and that white front door. My enemies are beyond this white lacquered door. I am holding the revolver tight with all the strength of my desperation. I am insane, I have shears to chop off anybody's future. I ring with insistence, I am sure if they get mad they will jump on me and it will be easier to pull out the gun and shoot them. I wait. Time goes by. Francesca is behind me and after a while she calls me gently with a thread of voice. I feel an idiot. I stand still in front of that closed door for ten minutes. My anger fades away overwhelmed by my good disposition. I would like to plunge in shame. Damn! Ridiculous in my anger, I am alone, snubbed by my enemies.

Somebody is pulling my arm. Francesca carries me away from that door that will never open for me. From the bridge of a small river, mirror of the sky, I throw the revolver into the water; I see it sinking down while the ripples dissolve the reflex of some clouds. I postpone my damnation and take my dignity back.

Some kids are playing loud at the public garden and their grandfathers look at them pleased. Thanks to them they will not completely die. Lucky them!

"But... Damn it!"

I can't refrain from cursing. I recognise the old man I met the first evening. I walk quickly towards him and by instinct I put my hand in my pocket looking for my revenge. He notices it, yet he does not run away.

"Stop!" he says in perfect Italian. I was not expecting this! "I know why you are here and I do not believe you will go further. However, if you have to, do not do it in front of my grandson. Be aware that you are alive only because of me…"

I see myself in his eyes and I find all my despair.

"We lost a son. It happened in the same moment and I have no consolation to know that mine killed yours. He grew up here, he lived and spoke as an Englishman. He and his wife were happy for this kid. It was enough for me. I didn't understand what was happening. Suddenly, he started travelling to Pakistan more often, until an Inspector of Scotland Yard knocked at my door. As you can see, we found out about it at the same time. I have been waiting for you since then. I knew you or somebody else would have asked for blood. I always paid my bills, you can collect now. I wasn't expecting an Italian to come first. I have worked in Italy for five years and I know Italians as good nature and indulgent people, *Inshallah*…"

I understand him, I would have reasoned just like him. I see him glorious as the dignity he is offering on his palm. His grandson has stopped swinging the swing. He listens to our conversation, curious about the weird language his grandfather speaks. He is so cute, he has a round face framed by curly hair. His eyes shine as the sea under the moon. I am about to take him up in my arms.

With an instinctive protective gesture, the grandfather prevents me from doing it. Then he lets me do it. I hug him tight and I hear his little heartbeat calling mine, lost ages ago. I feel disgusted by revenge, wars, bombs and death. Then I have an absurd idea!

"Let me grow him up as he is my son. This will be the ransom for our lost lives," I tell him without hope.

This pending silence has a sweet taste, I couldn't

say why.

Then: "His mother is under psychiatric treatments. She attempted suicide for the disgrace. I cannot count on her, I will think about it…"

He is a wise man, he firmly looks at me straight into the eyes, maybe to bind me to a silent oath. There is not much more to say.

"I am planning to go back to Italy soon. I will wait for you in London for a few more days. I will never come back here, that's for sure. You shall look for me."

I am about to give him my address but I do not do it. They beat me a few steps from there, he can ask them where to find me. This is the end of the conversation.

I don't even look at Francesca. I wish I could escape any attention! I forget the hate, the anger and a revolver at the bottom of the river. Only my sorrow is burning as the sun at its zenith.

No one will ever come to me.

91

August 2006

(6th August, 2006)

I have my Alitalia ticket. Date, time and gate already printed. The Chinese man of the pizzeria hugged me and he was moved. Kneading pizzas made him a little Italian. He even paid the "payout" for my moonlighting. I didn't expect it. I spend the last days at the Thames' banks. I don't like this river with muddy water. I lean my surly thoughts on it, but the water is so slow that does not dissipate them.

I wonder whether I was a good father to Paolo. Undoubtedly, I want to be worthy of his memory. Not being guilty of any crime is the best way to start. I pluck up the courage...

I smile and even the Thames has a golden light under the sunshine brush. I look at it for the last time; I will take the plane in the afternoon.

There is no essence in my sighs; revenge is not accomplished. I think of Mohamed Khan's father, his elegant but sad appearance, his broken dream, his sorrow so identical to mine, his relief identical to my vengeance, and I am not surprised to see him coming. He came to mine conclusions. His grandson hugs him tightly by the neck. I envy him. He is not in a hurry, neither am I. We have a mindful gentlemen's agreement to fulfil a difficult and honest task. Growing a man who is able to be Kaled and understand Paolo's culture. I want a son back. Neither a hostage nor a pledge. Francesca is looking at us far away, respecting our privacy. We do not have many words to say. We do not need them.

"Take him away from here, fanatical believers will treat him as a symbol, as the son of a martyr, for English people he will be always a terrorist's son... This must not happen. I beg you, let him have a honourable life..." Then he gives me the kid. I haven't felt such a deep tenderness for a long time.

"Here's the uncle that grandpa was telling you about..." I believe these are the words he gently whispers to him. Then he lets go his neck and grabs mine. He is holding me tightly. I could remain like this for the rest of my life. His small hands are touching with curiosity the veins of my neck, swollen by the effort of restraining tears. I love him already, this takes me even more away from his father who "decided" not to see him ever again.

(7th August, 2006)

The return journey. I am holding again my little Paolo in my arms, this means he never left. I feel invincible. I forget the blows received. Finally at home. Here, for the last time I breathe that indefinite feeling of things not completely dead. I feel every hanging drop of sadness that I lived. I do not want my little guest to breathe it. I open the shutters that strongly slam, I let the sun kill the bad thoughts hidden in the shadow. Kaled smiles quietly. This is the best gift. He is curious to discover the house. He touches things and lifts them up over his head to measure them. It only takes a few hours to be at his ease, it seems he has always lived here. Then I go upstairs in the bedroom and on the unmade bed, I find Lucia's letter. She slept here. She used to do it when she wanted to tell me something important. She used to write on a paper and leave it where I could find it at night. I am so much marked by the recent events that I can't help being anxious. Just a few words, it is a meagre invitation.

"Roberto, I would like to see you, to talk as we used to in the past. Francesca informed me of everything without your knowledge. I work at the old church of Divino Amore. Let me know when you come so I free myself. I will wait for you."

I organise for the following morning. I want to see her too. Then I call Francesca, our evolved relationship is reassuring me.

"Can you come over tomorrow so Pa...sorry, Kaled will not be alone?"

I am collecting hours of friendship to change that sole night of sex into a memory lost in our common moments.

(21st August, 2006)

The church is cool inside. I am at my ease while Lucia is coming toward me. It is so beautiful to see her smile. She kisses my lips as a sister, but I feel something more. I hug her in the sacred silence of the liturgies lived here, a gesture that dispels our anxiety.

"How is your job?"

She is pleased for that question. However, it is only courtesy. We are able to keep Paolo out of the conversation. She is so beautiful caressed by time. Small wrinkles around the eyes are like sunbeams. She is more fascinating now that she smiles with grace without losing sight of me. While we talk, the keeper comes with a dusty bottle and time is like an oyster with a pearl inside. The ruby colour of wine is an alchemy's secret.

What a good feeling having met Lucia again after so many years. I live the intensity of her eyes regardless of the boasting tales of the pouring wine. This man does not exist between us, he is a "serf" coming out from the ancestral shadow of the church. His slow movements are annoying me. I do not like his sloppy presence, however I do not want him to notice it. Actually, I wonder how he is fine with such a beautiful woman as Lucia next to him. Then the wine adjusts sunshine and shadow while its flavour spreads in the air. We toast touching our glasses before drinking. The perfect occasion to exchange our loving glances. Lucia is better than me in interweaving conversation. She talks to me about him and vice versa with great consideration. I haven't understood the reason I was there until the wine came out. The tapster is a detail. Her gentle solicitude to make me drink that nectar is such a delicacy. My passion grows among the plies of her lips. I am her accomplice. I let her lead me. Today I have no drama, I have no history. It is only her and her desires.

At the restaurant she has assumed a vestal modesty. I have to insist to make her eat. I like to see her doing such an alive gesture. She talks about her projects while her impeccable hands are swirling in the air. I am crazy about her. We remain seated for a little, I want to disclose my love with the dignity of my adult age. I pay attention not to claim anything. I am aware that longing for a dreamed love is fascination; its existence is a fatal decline. We are at her house. I hope she doesn't say good-bye here, I wouldn't want to. I feel my body is stretching out until it hurts. I must touch her skin that will feel my vibes. She lets me kiss her. I am not shamed this time, not at all. There is no reason to hide my excitement as I get closer to her womb. I finally hear her "yes" howled in the silence of our kisses. Her saliva is sea-foam that washes my beach. We go upstairs. I push her on the bed whereas the body opposes a fake resistance. I get undressed. I want her to be in front of a clear signal. There aren't important things to say, never more important than the gestures of our bodies. Our hands feel the heat of our skin, my mouth is eager for her deep breaths of pleasure. Around, the afternoon fades away the sunbeams until they disappear in the corners of the room. At night, everything has a dark gold colour around me. Now I know I have

just lived a dream and I wish I could deserve it again!
The turned on radio is broadcasting a beautiful song by
Don Backy...

"I look up at the sky and I see clusters of gold stars,

they are my life, by now ended, by now ended if you are not with me...

The dawn will come, the night will go away

and the sun will unveil millions of things

together with us.

Stay with me, never leave me,

you are the only reason of my life,

let me live.

Mountains full of light I will search for you,

only for you.

Green tales of love I write for you.

You are for me, my dream of love,

something that lasts for life,

beyond life..."

(SOGNO, 1968)

I wish I had written it. I dedicate it to her.

I have not enough of her body but I check my impulse. She looks at me from her side of the bed. She lights a cigarette.

I get up for a glass of water but her words let me forget it.

"I leave. I signed a contract for South America, I will stay away for a long time."

Here again, our future slips out of our hands, like

the sand of some beaches. I was not expecting it to hurt me so much. I feel my blood frozen in my veins. I am about to faint, I sit.

"You do the right thing, it is your life." I am not happy. I have never learnt to hide my emotions, today I don't make exception. However, I believe she has accepted my words. She does not ask me anything else, she does not want to deepen the conversation. She just let me go. I am not turning back. I switch the radio on while in the car. I don't want to listen to the sound of shattered dreams inside me ever again.

March 2025

(March 2025)

...If I could had written a script of my life, "that" would have been our last encounter. But it was not. We met some other times. At the graveyard for the anniversaries of our son's death. I saw her talking to the picture while caressing his face. Her soft hands with tapering fingers were the love of an embarrassed mother and her tenderness wrung my heart. The truth is that I loved her as she was – busy and away. One night we had dinner together. She was always in a rush and her kisses tasted like other countries, may be other men, it's better let it go. I am still very fond of her! I can tell it now after a long time. Now that words are spoken at my sick-bed.

Time is so weird, it is so heavy on the skin, so light when it fades away from you. It has odd shapes, either round as a coloured balloon or sharp as a Toledo blade. Since then I counted nineteen years. All these years I have never stopped longing for death, yet as a secondary choice.

I brought up my second son with happiness. I look at him while he is sleeping on a chair at the bottom of my bed in the hospital. Behind his closed and peaceful eyes, I know there is a good heart, a "gentleman". I love him as much as I loved Paolo. The spirit of God is granting me a few more hours to cry the last tears of joy. We have just celebrated his degree in Medicine. We already knew about my illness. We chose not to tell anyone. It was our secret. He has lived these last few months with the prostration of losing a father, and this makes me proud. Every day I have feared to lose him and it couldn't be otherwise.

The loss of Paolo has been so piercing that will never heal. I am sorry he has breathed it.

He did more than his duty. He spent his youth closed at home studying. Yet he lived it like a "chrysalis". A longer effort to change into a more beautiful butterfly. He is a doctor now and I hope he will save so many lives to make forget the ones his father pulled away from the earth. Meanwhile, terrorist attacks are still happening. Their actions are quick to not realise they are on the wrong side. Ideas supported by exploding bombs. What a shame! Then when the noise is over and the dust of the explosions falls to the ground, nothing remains of their reasons, just the victims' forefinger pointing at them. In the silence of the obscurity, a radio broadcasts some classic music. I relax. I pray for this night to be the longest in my 73 years, I want to finish this diary. It is my only heritage, the one that I couldn't have left to Paolo. For all these years, I have treasured magnificent words to use on my "deathbed". Finally, here comes my ideal condition!!! I am so close to God's mercy, so far from human hate. The "deathbed", the deck of a ship on a stormy sea. A privileged position to look at the horizon, while its head is following the ship's course, a fulfilled destiny. They considered the "deathbed" as the last heartbeat, a breath broken among the teeth, the lowest point of the setting sun. Now I know it is not like that!

It is the fifth season of our life. It is the shortest, the most intense.

I am fully aware of it. I thank God! I feel more responsible after the old Pakistani's death. At his funeral his peaceful expression clashed with the shouting of the restless relatives all around. My Kaled had a dignified behaviour. He kept away from that "bailamme". Sad and engrossed in his thoughts, he was holding his grandfather's hand. I was standing aside while watching him. I loved him so much as my son that I was feeling compensated. I did not care if others' looks were hostile; I was there to honour an authentic man. He had fought for his belief until his death, pointing at me while telling him: "Here's your father."

Such a manly touch secured my old age. I was grateful to him!

I was longing for this from the bottom of my heart, since our first meeting at the park. Now I know! My dreaming time is over! What a pity! I was inattentive.

I need to hurry, my illness is jeopardizing my judgment. My sight is getting weak and dim, I barely see the difference between morning and night. I wish I could live one more day. My skin is stretched over my bones frame, like the wind-vanes in *Don Quixote*. How I wish the wind would pierce me, make me live that vertigo that lets you fly, fill the wings and go away...

"Kaled, please take me to the balcony, I need some fresh air."

"Pa, you know it is not good for you, you are not feeling well to get out."

"My beloved son, this is the last favour. Believe

me, they will be minutes spent well."

Since I look like a wind-vane I want my portion of air and I want my flight! His strong arms lifts me up like a sail on the mainmast. I feel good in the outline of his hug. I have the taste of the wind on my lips, finally my best smile is arising. Lucia arrives just when my life is fading away. Her kiss on my forehead is the polar star over my quiet sea. I let things around slide away and I am happy now I hear Kaled crying!

"Here's the good man that I promised You when Paolo was born. Here's my gift, God!"

Finally, God's reply comes. While I am leaving forever no one bomb explodes in this world…no one rose is bathed in blood.

Blood of scarlet rose

Index

July-August 2005	5
Ottobre 2005	15
November-December 2005	21
January 2006	37
March 2006	51
April 2006	55
May 2006	63
June 2006	69
July 2006	77
August 2006	91
March 2025	101
Index	**109**

9 781911 424826